W9-BMQ-435

This Ladybird book
belongs to

. . . .

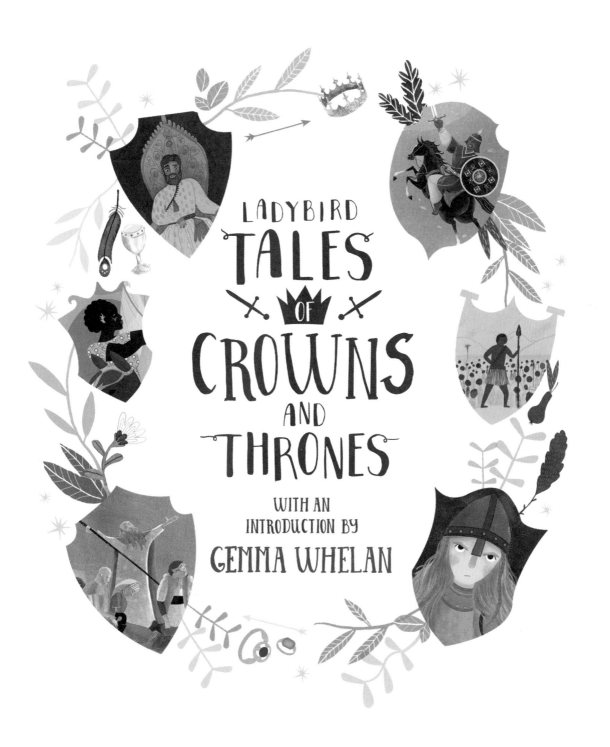

LADYBIRD
TALES
OF
CROWNS
AND
THRONES

WITH AN
INTRODUCTION BY
GEMMA WHELAN

CONTENTS

INTRODUCTION

"When I was little, I would often play with my brother and cousins. We would create magical worlds of knights and dragons and dress up as queens and kings, swishing around in my mum's old nighties and my dad's old velvet jacket. We would lord it up and order each other around in our elaborate, imaginary kingdoms.

As we grew up, my brother and cousins became serious adults with "proper jobs". But, I refused to leave the enchanting world of make-believe. I danced, sang, played and now I perform as different characters on the stage and TV. I dress up for a living!

One character I played was a seafaring warrior queen called Yara. She was fierce and strong, but also very loyal, courageous and fair – much like the princesses you will meet in this book.

Yara didn't wear fancy clothes or drink tea and eat scones in the afternoon. She didn't attend ballroom dances, and she certainly didn't wait around for a handsome prince to come along and sweep her off her feet.

Yara was so busy being herself, and following her dreams, that she hardly had time to wash! But she shone because she was true to herself, she knew who she was and what she wanted and she wasn't afraid to go after it. She listened to her heart, that quiet place inside her that spoke the truth to her soul and guided her on her path.

I believe that this is what it truly means to be a king or queen. By treating people with kindness and respect – from friends and family to strangers and even people we don't like – we can be as regal and heroic as Rostam, Shakuntala or Gwendolyn from these stories. If we choose love, first for ourselves and then for others, and if we behave with honour and dignity, then we are all monarchs! Wherever we sit, that is our throne and wherever we wander, that is our kingdom.

So happy reading, dear fellow queens and kings, princes and princesses, and remember – whether you live in a castle or a house or even on the streets, we are all equal. To treat people equally is my golden rule for every ruler.

Gemma Whelan

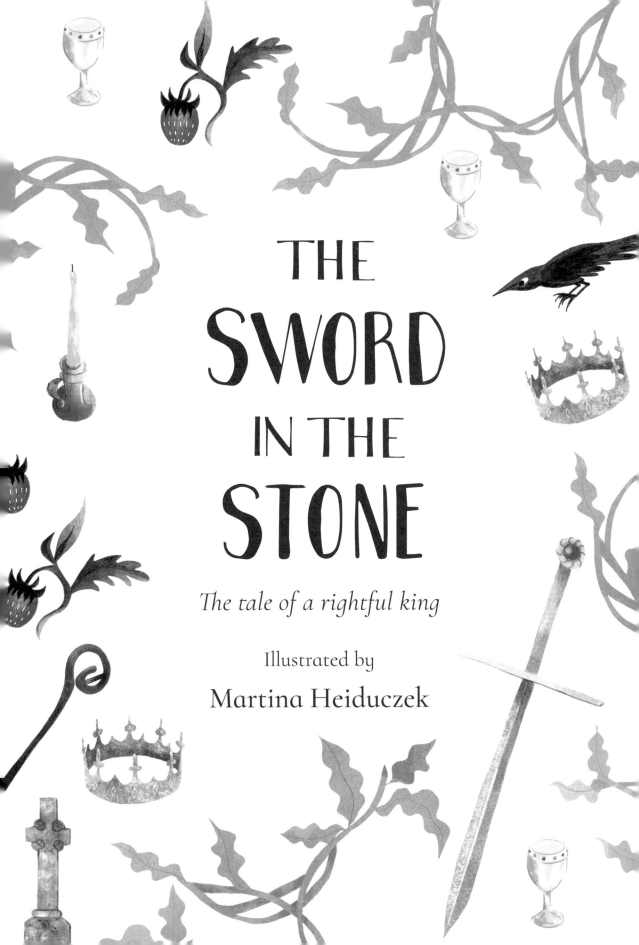

THE
SWORD
IN THE
STONE

The tale of a rightful king

Illustrated by

Martina Heiduczek

King Uther had almost everything a king could want. He had the love and respect of his people. He had riches and health. He had Merlin, the great sorcerer, to advise him. But King Uther was not happy.

"Merlin." He sighed. "I've brought peace to the land and yet I am not at peace."

"What troubles you?" the sorcerer replied.

"I want a queen to share my throne and a child to share my heart. I need a son who will inherit my crown, continue serving my people and keep peace in my kingdom."

Merlin agreed to help the king, but he had one condition. "I will help you find a queen, Uther, but I need you to prove your trust in me. You must give me your firstborn child."

Taken aback by his advisor's request, the king reluctantly agreed. Though he dearly wanted a son, he could think of nothing but the happiness he would share with his future bride. Merlin soon discovered the whereabouts of the king's soulmate and, a short time later, King Uther married Lady Ygraine.

After months of pure happiness, King Uther and Queen Ygraine welcomed their son, Arthur. The kingdom erupted in celebration, but Merlin made Uther keep his word. Merlin took the baby and placed him in the care of Sir Ector, an ally of the king, who promised to care for the boy, not knowing that this baby was the heir to the throne.

As time went on, King Uther became sick. He was so sick that even Merlin's magic could not save him. From his deathbed, he asked one final favour of his friend.

"Promise me, dear Merlin, that you will look after my people when I am gone. That you will find someone worthy of the crown, who will protect and guide the kingdom."

"I promise," the sorcerer replied.

When Uther died, the kingdom fell into despair. Panic rippled through the kingdom as everyone suddenly thought that they were worthy to wear the crown.

The would-be rulers argued and fought between themselves, creating rebellions, war and unrest. The peace that King Uther had worked so hard to protect was starting to unravel. The people turned to Merlin for help.

"Merlin!" they cried. "You have the wisdom of the stars and can conduct such powerful magic. Surely you can decide who among us is worthy of taking Uther's place as king?"

"I will not choose a ruler," the sorcerer told the disappointed crowd. "It is for fate, not man, to decide."

What Merlin needed most was time – he knew that once Arthur had fully grown, he would be able to claim the crown as his own. But that would take a few more years. So the wise sorcerer devised a plan.

"Tell your noblemen to meet me in the churchyard in three days' time. There, I will set a test that only the true king will be able to complete."

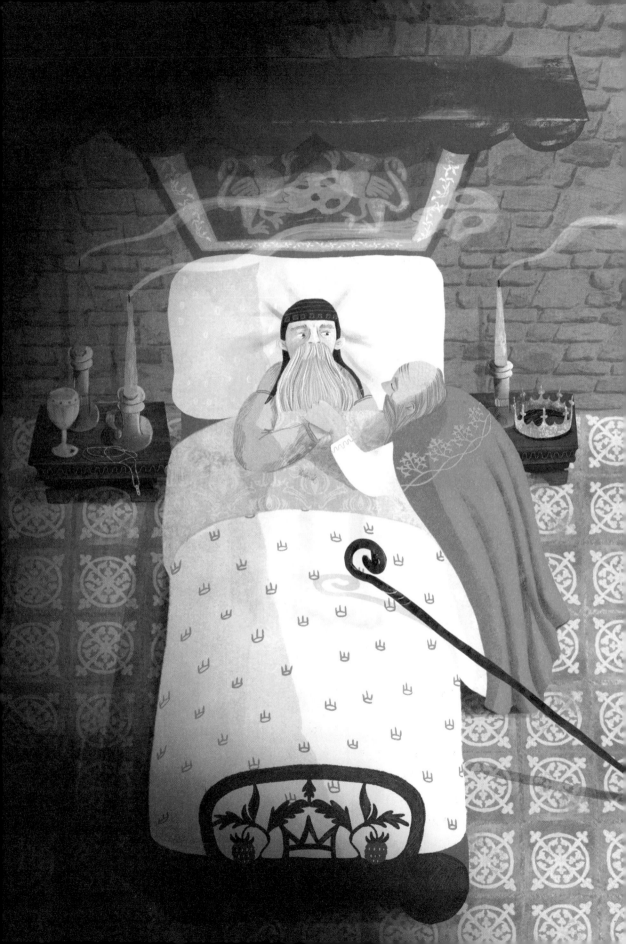

Three days later, all the would-be rulers gathered in the churchyard to hear how they could prove their worth. Would Merlin set a difficult quest to test their bravery? Or perhaps a tournament to test their skills in battle?

After much debate, Merlin appeared and called everyone round a large stone in the middle of the churchyard. On top of the stone, he set an anvil and, within the anvil, he had magically placed a sword.

"Only the one who is worthy to wear the crown," he explained, "will be able to pull this sword from the stone."

The noblemen looked at each other in disbelief – was that all? It didn't seem like much of a competition, but they trusted Merlin and so formed a line to try one by one. Each nobleman thought himself more worthy than the last. But they all failed. They saw for themselves that it was impossible. They were not worthy.

For years, knights protected the sword day and night, as people travelled from across the land to try and remove the sword from the stone. Men and women of all shapes and sizes tried to prove their strength by yanking the sword free. They all failed. Some studied the angle and weight, the direction of the wind and size, trying to use science to pull the sword free. They failed, too.

Only Merlin knew that Arthur, the rightful heir, would come to pull the sword from its stony prison when the time was right.

As noblemen from around the country tried to prove their worth, Arthur grew up in the house of Sir Ector. But life was hard. Ector and his wife had promised Merlin that they would keep the baby safe and raise him as if he was their own, but they were unkind to the boy.

They treated Arthur as though he were a servant. They sent him out on errands and made him clean the yard, fetch and carry supplies and work in the garden.

Nothing Arthur did was good enough. There was always something more to do. If he was tired from a long day of doing everyone else's chores, they called him lazy. If he finished his work quickly and treated himself to a walk outside, they called him idle. Even Ector's son, Sir Kay, teased Arthur day and night.

"I don't know why my father agreed to take in such a skinny, useless worm as you," he shouted at Arthur. "What a waste of space! You'll never amount to much. You won't even be fit to lick my boots when I grow up and take over."

Arthur spent most of his time alone and grew up as a very lonely boy. When he was afforded any time to himself, he would turn to his beloved books, talk to the horses in the stables or walk the fields and woodlands for fresh air – anything to escape the insults and orders from Sir Ector and his family. Arthur would often disappear into his daydreams, wondering if he was destined for something greater.

One day, Sir Kay and his friends became bored while stalking rabbits in the fields and decided to make Arthur the new target of their hunt. As they raced around the fields, Arthur waited quietly in the woods, watching.

Suddenly, a mysterious man appeared next to the young king. He looked familiar, but Arthur wasn't sure where he had seen the man's face before.

"What are you doing here, boy?" the man asked.

Soothed by his kind voice, Arthur stopped to reply. "Just waiting. They'll soon grow tired of looking for me."

"You could throw one of these rotten apples at them?"

Arthur shook his head.

"I could turn them into something for you," the man suggested. "A frog, maybe? Or perhaps a rat?"

Arthur laughed. "No, it's OK. It wouldn't be fair to punish someone who doesn't know any better."

Merlin was impressed by Arthur's good nature. He knew he had made the right choice for the boy. The young king was developing a kind heart in spite of his circumstances.

From that moment, Merlin visited Arthur as often as he could. He taught him about the world, using nature and the stars, and told him tales of magic, miracles, travel and hope. Arthur grew to be kind, adventurous, noble, curious, courageous and honest. Merlin taught Arthur not only the character of a king, but also of a great ruler. Soon it was clear that it was time to take him to the stone.

Once more, Merlin gathered the nobles to the stone in the churchyard. This time he invited Sir Ector, Sir Kay and Arthur to come along as well.

"I can't wait to see you all kneel before me!" Sir Kay boasted as he approached the sword.

He pulled.

Nothing happened.

He pulled again, this time harder. Again, nothing happened.

"What a stupid test," Kay declared, his pride quite broken. "No one could pull that thing out."

"Perhaps the other young man would like to try?" Merlin asked calmly, pointing to the timid Arthur.

"Him?" Sir Ector exclaimed. "He can barely pull my horse!"

"Strength is more than just brute force," Merlin replied, waving Arthur towards the stone. "A strong character can be just as effective and is even more important."

Arthur approached the stone with little expectation but, as he put his fingers on the hilt, he felt a surge of magic run through him. Then he pulled.

All but Merlin were shocked to see the sword slide easily from the stone. As Arthur raised the blade high above his head, the watching crowd sank to their knees to bow before their new king. The lost son of Uther had proved he was worthy of the sword and the crown. He would rule the kingdom with a kind heart and fair hand, just as Merlin had foreseen.

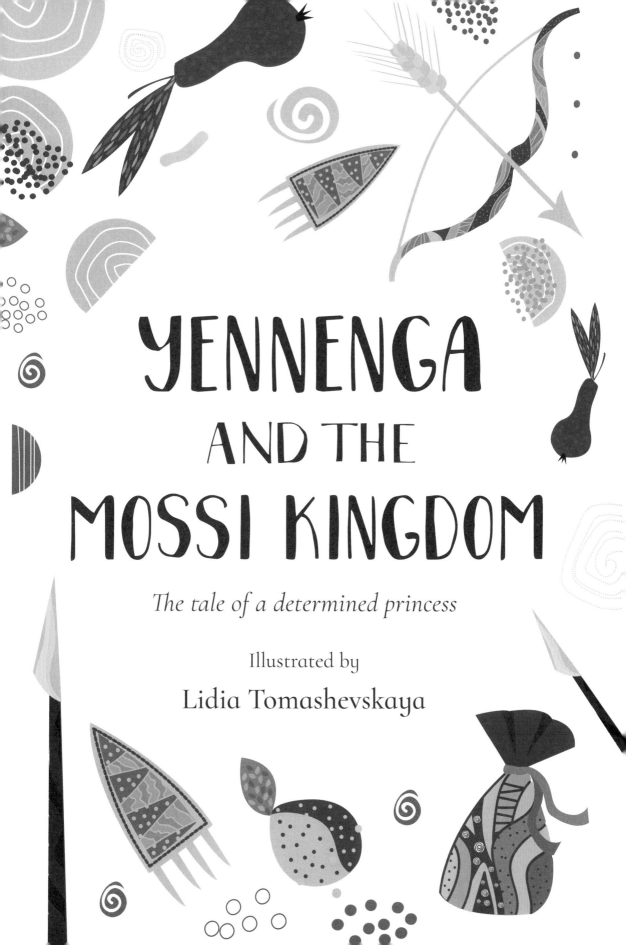

YENNENGA
AND THE
MOSSI KINGDOM

The tale of a determined princess

Illustrated by

Lidia Tomashevskaya

rom a very young age, Princess Yennenga was beloved by the Dagomba people. Her father, King Nedega, taught her that a kingdom is more than just land and wealth – a kingdom is the people. So, as a young girl, the princess would regularly go out to help her community.

"How may I lighten your load, dear friend?" she would ask her neighbours, friends and family. The Dagomba would often see Yennenga fetching water, looking after younger children, sewing garments or carrying goods. She was particularly talented at working the fields. Yennenga loved to see crops flourish and she could turn dry, weed-ridden patches of scrubland into lush, fruitful fields for all to share. The princess had the magic touch!

When she wasn't tending crops, helping people or playing with her friends and brothers, the princess spent time with her beloved horse. Yennenga was an excellent rider and she trained her stallion as hard as she trained herself. Both princess and horse raced as one, moving swiftly and gracefully.

"I don't know why you train so hard," her brothers would tease. "Father will never let you on to the battlefield. Your place is here, at home."

Yennenga ignored her brothers' taunts and she soon became the fastest rider in the Dagbon Kingdom. She practised fighting with javelins, spears and bows, and it wasn't long before her dedication to training caught her father's eye.

When she became a teenager, Princess Yennenga approached her father for permission to protect the people she had come to love so dearly.

"Father, the Malinke tribe get closer every day and we must protect our land. As your fastest rider and fiercest fighter, please allow me to fight for our people's safety."

The king thought long and hard about what his daughter was asking. She was the most dedicated in training and much stronger than her brothers, but she was also the most caring towards her subjects.

"Who will care for the people if you are on the battlefield with me?" he asked.

"Who will care for the people if we lose the fight?" she replied.

From that day forward, Yennenga fought alongside her father in battles, proving her skill and bravery many times. The sight of the princess on the back of her mighty stallion, bow drawn, sent fear into the hearts of her enemies.

Yennenga's reputation as a fierce warrior spread beyond the kingdom. It wasn't long before she was in command of her own battalion, and she led them to victory after victory.

Her father could not imagine life without his most valued commander, and he would send Yennenga and her battalion to lands far away in search of further glory.

Soon Princess Yennenga was tired of war and she longed for her home. She wanted to return to help her people again, just as she had as a little girl, so she appealed to the king.

"Father, I have done all you have asked of me on the field of battle. The threat from the Malinke tribe is over," she said. "It is time for me to put down my sword."

King Nedega became angry. "You, who have led warriors to battle wish to abandon your post? You, who have made barren lands plentiful, would now leave them unprotected?"

"Father, my brothers will take over my battalion. I want to return to care for the people I fought for."

"No," he replied. "My need of your service is greater than theirs. Never speak of this again."

For years, Yennenga tried to persuade her father to let her come home, but he would not change his mind. So she planted a field of wheat outside his front door and, when it grew lush and full, she refused to harvest it. Then, when it began to wilt and die, still she would not harvest it.

"Why would you waste food so carelessly when you know our people need to eat?" King Nedega barked at his daughter.

The princess replied calmly, "Our people are like the wheat and your stubbornness means that I have no choice but to leave them to perish."

Enraged, the king locked Yennenga away. He hoped she would change her mind and behave, and he told himself that this was the one battle the princess could not win.

28

Days, weeks and months passed, but still the princess and the king could not come to an agreement.

Just as Yennenga started to fear that she may never be free, she heard a familiar voice at her prison door. "Princess, I cannot bear to leave you here to rot another day. You have done so much for us. Our people *must* see you freed."

The voice belonged to her friend, one of the king's horsemen. He had risked everything to come and see Yennenga. The princess recognized the horseman's bravery and knew that this was her only chance to escape. All that she had achieved would mean nothing if her people did not see her win her freedom. Together, they formed a plan.

The next night, Yennenga waited in her cell until she heard a click in the lock. The horseman had stolen the key from the guard. As the door creaked open, Yennenga's friend flung a bag into the cell. There were clothes inside and the princess put them on, transforming herself into a stable boy.

They walked across the courtyard to the stables, where two horses, including Yennenga's trusty stallion, were saddled and ready to go. They mounted their steeds and raced off into the night.

As they galloped into the darkness, the princess knew it would be a long time before she would be able to return home. She would miss her father and her brothers and, most of all, her people, but Yennenga knew in her heart that the only way to find freedom was to leave.

Yennenga and the horseman rode for many days to put as much distance between themselves and the Dagbon Kingdom as they could. Yennenga travelled in her disguise, just in case she was spotted and sent back to her prison, but the wrath of her father was not her only worry.

The two friends had ridden so far that they found themselves in the territory of the Malinke tribe. It wasn't long before patrolling Malinke warriors saw them. The warriors set up an ambush and, although outnumbered, the friends fought bravely. The horseman was injured in the middle of a swift attack, and he gave his life to protect the princess. In a fit of rage and revenge, Yennenga swung her sword and defeated her enemies.

Tired but forced to continue her journey, Yennenga travelled on alone. She rode for many days and many nights until she became unsure of where she was.

"We're lost," the princess whispered to her horse. She had no food or water. It had been days since she had passed a river or a stream. The land was unfamiliar and, for once, she could not trust it to feed her.

On she rode, deep into the heart of a forest. Yennenga was so exhausted from her journey that she was in danger of falling off her horse. As her tired body began to slide from the saddle, she felt two strong arms guide her to the ground and a blanket was wrapped round her.

The next morning, Yennenga woke to the sound of a campfire and the smell of porridge. Unsure whether the man offering her breakfast was friend or foe, Yennenga decided to stay in disguise until she knew she was safe.

"My name is Riale," he said as he handed her a bowl. "I am just an elephant hunter so I don't have much, but what I have, I can share with you."

Riale and Yennenga kept one another company, growing closer as the days passed. They told tales of adventures, home and growing up and, evenutally, they fell in love. It was time for Princess Yennenga to tell Riale the truth.

"If we are to be equals, you must know who I am," she said. "I am the runaway princess of the Dagbon Kingdom. I left because my father would not let me look after my people. It was only through their kindness that I was able to escape, but I fear I may never return."

Touched by her story, Riale vowed to stand by his princess. Together, they made decisions as a team and they respected each other's strength and wisdom.

The two went on to marry and, later, they had a son, who they named Ouedragogo. Ouedragogo inherited skills, intelligence, bravery and creativity from both of his parents. He grew up respecting others and the land around him. Eventually, Ouedragogo would establish the Mossi Kingdom, making Princess Yennenga – warrior, commander and horsewoman – the mother of the Mossi Kingdom.

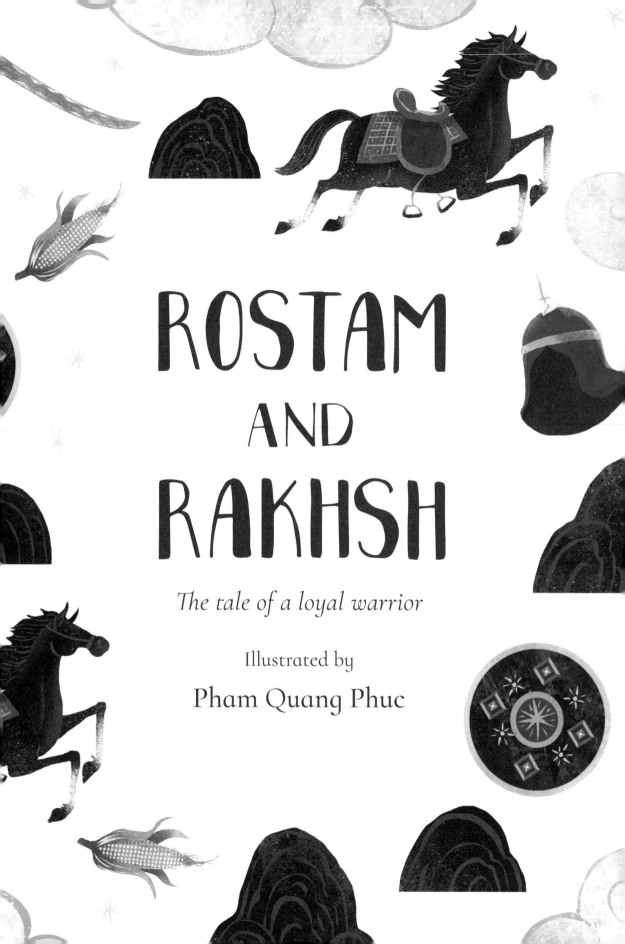

ROSTAM
AND
RAKHSH

The tale of a loyal warrior

Illustrated by

Pham Quang Phuc

Rostam the warrior was tall, broad-shouldered and brave. He was the son of Zal, the great protector of King Kavus, the king of Persia. When Zal gifted Rostam a mighty horse called Rakhsh, he said, "Be prepared to always serve the throne of Persia with loyalty and courage."

Rostam grew up during a peaceful time in Persia and was yet to experience war. But things changed when King Kavus decided to attack Mazanderan, the land of demons.

"Fighting evil magic with iron swords is a fool's errand," warned Zal, but King Kavus ignored his old protector's advice. The king summoned an army and travelled to Mazanderan, where he fought a great battle. But the king lost. The White Demon, who stood guard at the entrance to Mazanderan, captured Kavus and blinded him.

When the king finally managed to send for help, Zal was deeply troubled. Fighting the White Demon was no task for an old man like him.

"Allow me to go instead, Father," Rostam said. Zal hesitated, for Rostam had never fought before. Zal was about to decline his son's request, when Rostam added, "With Rakhsh at my side, I'll return victorious. I know I will." Seeing the determination in his son's eyes, Zal agreed.

The route through forest and desert lands to the kingdom of Mazanderan was the most direct, but it was also the most dangerous. Rostam and Rakhsh rode for many days until they finally found a spot in the forest to rest.

Tired from the journey, Rostam slept soundly, while his horse kept watch. As night drew in and the forest became darker, Rakhsh heard a low growl.

A lion crouched nearby, ready to pounce. Without hesitation, Rakhsh charged at the lion. He kicked the lion in the face and scared it off into the trees. His friend was safe. When Rostam woke up, he thanked Rakhsh for saving his life, but he was also angry.

"What if the lion had attacked you, Rakhsh? Please wake me next time," he urged. "We are stronger together."

Leaving the forest behind, they rode through a vast desert. The day grew hotter as the sun rose. Rostam's throat was parched and his flask was empty. Unable to ride any further, Rostam dropped to his knees and prayed to God.

"Please help me find water," he begged. "I do not want to fail in my mission. The king and my father are depending on me to succeed."

When Rostam opened his eyes, a ram stood in front of him. The weary travellers followed the sheep until it eventually led them to a stream. Rostam and Rakhsh drank their fill and found the strength to continue their journey.

Another night, Rostam found a spot in the desert to sleep. In the darkest hour, a small but fierce dragon crept close. Panicked, Rakhsh nudged Rostam awake. But as soon as Rostam sat up, the dragon disappeared.

"You're imagining things," Rostam told Rakhsh. "Let me sleep."

But soon, the dragon returned. Despite Rostam's request, Rakhsh neighed loudly to alert his master and, in the dim light of dawn, Rostam finally spotted the dragon and slayed it.

He thanked Rakhsh and gratefully patted the horse.

They resumed their journey, speeding through the endless desert. They came upon an oasis full of delicious food and drink. Thanking his good fortune, Rostam ate a hearty meal and sang the songs his mother had taught him.

"Such a sweet voice," cried an evil witch, listening nearby. "I must make its owner my slave."

Dressed as a beautiful woman, the witch tracked down the travellers and approached Rostam. He kindly offered her some food and sat down to share a meal with his new companion.

"Let's thank God for all his kindness," Rostam prayed.

The name of God broke the witch's spell, revealing her true form. Rostam quickly jumped up. He charged at the evil witch and ran his sword through her heart.

"We must not rest until we reach Mazanderan," Rostam vowed as they resumed their journey.

The next evening, under the cover of a darkening sky, Rostam reached a field of corn. Hungry and tired, he quickly jumped the fence to pick a few ears of the golden corn. He did not think who the field might belong to.

"Stop!" a voice cried out. "How dare you steal *my* corn!"

Rostam tried to reason with the farmer, Olad. But Olad was in no mood to listen. Despite Rostam's pleading, Olad refused to accept his apology, so Rostam picked up the farmer and tied him to a tree.

Fearing the worst, the farmer cried out. "Please spare me! I was only trying to protect my crops. If you let me down, I can lead you to Mazanderan. I know how to defeat the White Demon." Rostam needed all the help he could get, so he carefully untied the farmer and held him to his word.

Olad led Rostam to the gatehouse on the outskirts of Mazanderan, guarded by the giant and fearsome Arzhang. Rostam jumped down from his horse, grabbed Arzhang by his ears and threw him beyond the boundaries. The rest of the guards ran in all directions, afraid of this seemingly fearless warrior.

It wasn't long before Rostam stumbled upon the prison of King Kavus. He paid the king his respects and Kavus was very happy indeed to hear Rostam's voice.

"Slay the White Demon in my name and bring his blood to cure my blindness," King Kavus ordered.

Rostam once again asked Olad for his help. "If we succeed, you will be rewarded well," he promised his new friend.

"You must wait for the sun to rise," advised Olad as Rostam sharpened his sword. "When the demons start falling asleep, kill them, then enter the White Demon's cave. He is almost impossible to kill, but you must hold your ground and wait for his moment of doubt."

Rostam was unable to sleep that night. He stayed awake and watched the demons until dawn broke and they began to fall asleep. He then made his way towards the entrance of the White Demon's cave, killing the drowsy guards easily with his sword.

Taking a deep breath, Rostam and Rakhsh entered the cave of the White Demon. There, as though he had been waiting for them to arrive, the demon stood. He was as big and dark as a stone mountain, and his hair was white under his golden helmet.

"For the honour of my king, I will kill you!" shouted Rostam, sitting up as tall as he could as he faced his foe.

The White Demon laughed. "That's impossible," he said. "Even though you have killed my guards, someone as small and weak as you could never achieve a glorious win against me."

Olad had warned Rostam of this moment. Without pausing even to take a breath, Rostam charged towards his enemy. Caught off guard, the White Demon was unable to mount a defence and Rostam killed him in an instant. He then gathered a cupful of the demon's blood to take back to King Kavus.

King Kavus was finally free and, with the blood from the White Demon, his sight was restored.

"It's time to return home," said Rostam. But King Kavus was stubborn. He saw an opportunity to stay and conquer Mazanderan after all. He taunted the king of demons to surrender.

"My warrior has defeated your White Demon and all of his guards," Kavus shouted to the demon king. "Your resistance is pointless. Surrender your kingdom to me."

But the king of demons was not willing to go down without a fight. Having defeated Arzhang and the White Demon, Rostam jumped on the back of Rakhsh and the two friends charged into the demon king's court.

Upon hearing the hooves of Rakhsh approaching, the terrified demon king turned into a mountain of stone so that Rostam would not be able to kill him.

"You cannot hide," Rostam shouted to the mountain. "I'll chip away at the rock with my axe and turn you into pebbles."

As Rostam raised his axe, the demon king surrendered. Rostam had saved the throne of Persia! With permission from the king, the loyal and trusted Olad was made the new protector and king of Mazanderan. Kavus and Rostam returned home with Rakhsh, triumphant and proud.

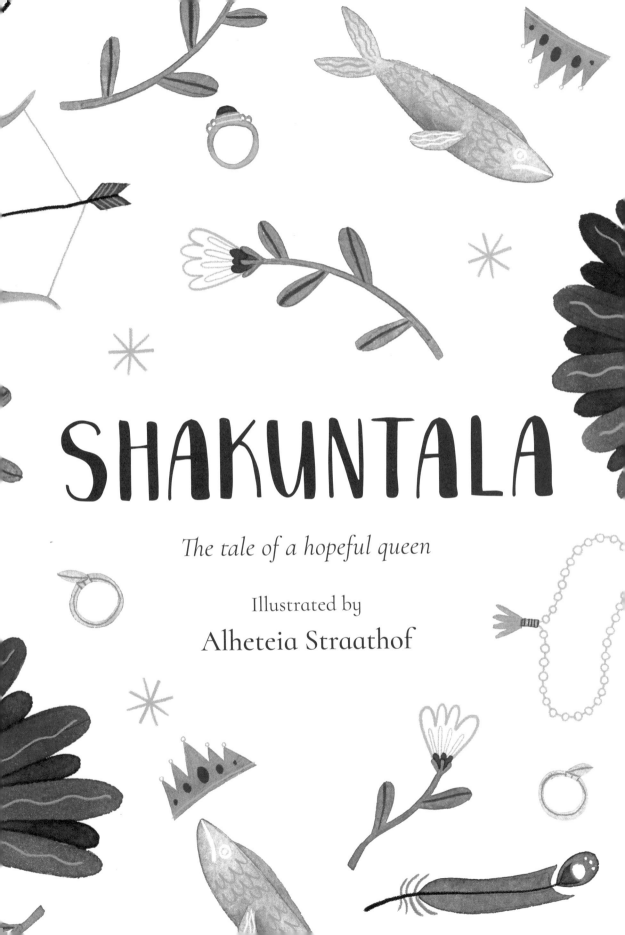

SHAKUNTALA

The tale of a hopeful queen

Illustrated by

Alheteia Straathof

As a baby, Shakuntala was found on the banks of the mighty river Ganga and, ever since, she had been bold and fearless. She grew up singing with the cuckoos and dancing with the peacocks. Her father, Sage Kanva, often said to her, "Be like the forest!"

Shakuntala became a kind, brave and hopeful young woman. "Nurture those who seek our refuge," her father advised her. "And always remain hopeful that light will come after darkness."

One afternoon, as Shakuntala was picking flowers, a deer sprinted towards her. A hunter followed on horseback, ready to shoot. Shakuntala sensed the danger to the animal and rushed in front of the charging horse.

"Stop!" she cried.

"Out of my way," replied the hunter angrily. "I am Dushyanta, the king of Hastinapura. Everything in this forest is mine. You have no right to stop me."

"A protector must not hunt his own subjects," argued Shakuntala boldly. She stood firmly in front of the horse. "You must nurture those who seek refuge."

King Dushyanta had never heard anyone speak to him this way and, as he let Shakuntala's words sink in, he realized she was right. "No one has ever pointed out my mistakes before," he said. "Please allow this ignorant king to apologize." Shakuntala accepted his humble apology and invited him to her home.

Shakuntala offered the king refreshments and they discussed
the beauty of the forest and the wonders of all the animals.
The king was so enchanted with this mysterious woman
that he stayed and spent the next few days getting to know
her. King Dushyanta had met many princesses before,
but none of them were as wise or as spirited as Shakuntala.

The day before the king was due to return to Hastinapura,
he proposed to Shakuntala. She agreed to marry him,
but only if he would make her three promises.

"Name them. I will do my best to make you happy,"
vowed the king.

"First, my son must inherit the throne," she said. "I'll raise
a prince worthy of ruling all the lands we can see, the rivers
that flow and the forests that grow."

"Of course! Our son will be the wisest king."

"Second, you will send me a wardrobe fit for a queen.
I live a humble life and will need to look like your queen."

"Done!" said Dushyanta.

"Third, you will marry me today, before you return.
The forest shall be our witness as my father is away."

"You strike a hard bargain," the king replied with a smile.
"But I accept."

So they married under the canopy of the forest branches.
The king gave Shakuntala his ring with the royal seal and
she gave him one made of holy grass.

After King Dushyanta returned to Hastinapura, Shakuntala began preparations for her journey to her new kingdom. She was so engrossed in her work that she didn't hear the footsteps approaching her front door.

Sage Durvasa, a wise rishi who lived near the forest, stood outside, tired and hungry. He was known for his short temper and powerful curses. He knocked and called out, but to no avail. Finally, Sage Durvasa shouted, "An unwelcoming house is worse than a bed of thorns!"

Startled by his harsh words, Shakuntala rushed outside to welcome the sage. But it was too late.

"You will be forgotten by your husband who has occupied your thoughts and caused such rude behaviour," the sage cursed angrily. Shakuntala was shocked. She had to find some way to reverse the curse. Her father's words echoed in her mind, "Light will come after darkness."

She took refreshments to the sage and apologized over and over again. Slowly, Durvasa's anger lessened as his hunger disappeared.

"I'm afraid I cannot take back my curse," said Durvasa. "Once a curse is made, it cannot be taken back, but it can be broken. If you were to show your husband an object he gave you, he will remember who you are."

Shakuntala touched the wedding ring on her finger. She hoped that it would be enough to break the curse.

When Shakuntala's father, Sage Kanva, returned, she told him about everything that had happened. She also revealed that she was pregnant with her husband's baby.

"You must tell the king at once," her father advised. "He cannot deny his wife and child."

The two set off for the capital, walking for many days through the forest before they finally reached the riverside.

A boatman offered to take them across the mighty river Ganga. It had been a very tiring journey and they were glad of the rest. Shakuntala bent to scoop some water from the river to wash her face. She was so tired that she didn't notice the wedding ring slip off her finger.

Outside the palace, there was a long queue to see the king. *Queens don't wait in line*, Shakuntala thought.

"Tell the king that his queen has arrived," she said to the palace guards. Confused but intrigued, King Dushyanta sent for her immediately.

"Who are you?" he asked. "How dare you call yourself my queen?" Of course, the king had not recognized her. The curse had come true.

"Show him the ring," Sage Kanva reminded her. Shakuntala held up her hand, but the ring was gone. Without the ring, there was no hope of breaking the curse.

Embarrassed, the two travellers were turned away from the palace immediately. *I must find the ring*, thought Shakuntala.

As Sage Kanva and Shakuntala reached the river on their journey home, Shakuntala suddenly remembered washing her face. She looked down into the depths of the water.

"It must have fallen in when I scooped a handful of water," she cried.

"This river flows from the ice-capped mountains down to the ocean," said the boatman. "If you lost something in the waters, you have lost it forever."

"I *will* find it," replied Shakuntala. "If not now, then some day."

Placing her trust in fate, Shakuntala and her father settled back into forest life and, months later, she gave birth to a son, Bharatha.

"I shall raise him as a prince," she said, "no matter what." Bharatha grew up bold and fearless, just like his mother.

Little did they know, the ring had sunk deep into the riverbed and was stuck between the rocks.

Many summers later, a featherback fish looking for food accidentally swallowed the ring. Weighed down by the gold, the fish was soon caught in a fisherman's net. As the fisherman cut his prize open, he found the golden ring inside.

"It's my lucky day," he said, recognizing the seal on the ring. He ran to the palace. "The king will surely reward me."

As soon as King Dushyanta was reunited with his ring, Durvasa's curse was broken. Memories of Shakuntala, the wedding and his promises flooded back to the king. He immediately ordered his horse to be brought to him.

"Follow me with a wardrobe fit for a queen," he commanded, recalling his second promise. "I am going on a journey to bring my wife home."

He soon came upon a clearing in the forest where a boy and a lion cub were playing together.

"Aren't you afraid?" the king asked the small child.

"Why should I be?" replied the boy curiously.

"What is your name?" asked the king.

"I'm Bharatha," said the boy. "I am the future king of all the lands we can see, the rivers that flow and the forests that grow."

The king's happiness knew no bounds. He was sure that Bharatha was Shakuntala's son. His own son. "Take me to your mother," he urged. As the king walked through the forest with his son, he was reminded of his visit all those years ago. He soon saw his lost wife through the trees and his heart was filled with joy.

"I never lost hope," Shakuntala cried as the king swung her up into his arms. "I knew the ring would be found."

King Dushyanta returned to Hastinapura with his queen and his prince. Their arrival was celebrated with much ceremony and glory. Prince Bharatha became the heir to the throne, just as Shakuntala had hoped.

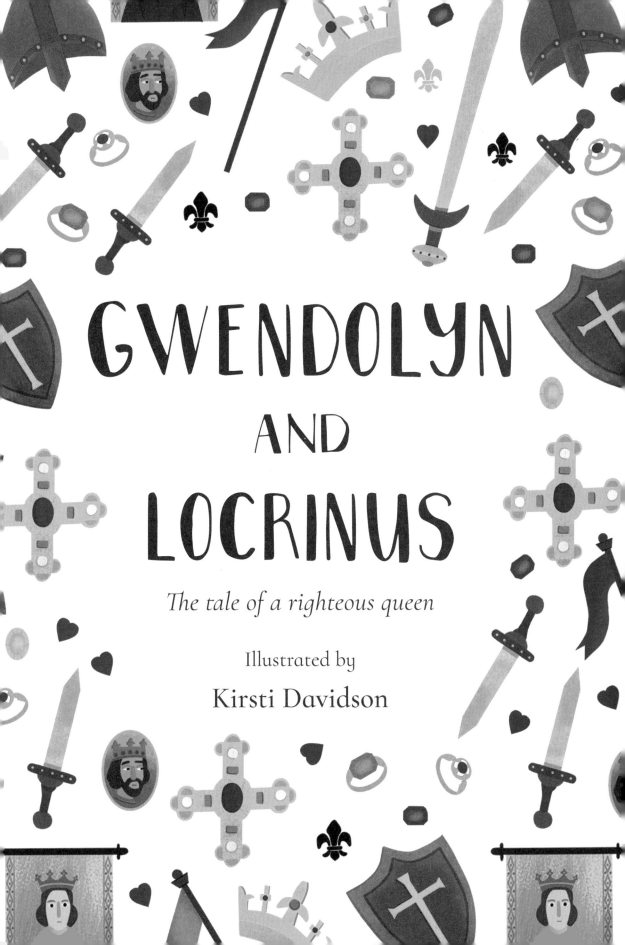

GWENDOLYN
AND
LOCRINUS

The tale of a righteous queen

Illustrated by

Kirsti Davidson

When Princess Gwendolyn was born, it was clear that she was as brave and courageous as her father, King Corineus of Cornwall, the slayer of giants.

"It's not the size of your enemy or their armies that matters," Gwendolyn's father told her as she jousted in the courtyard and fenced through the Great Hall. "It is your courage that will win battles."

When the time came for Gwendolyn to be married, her father suggested she marry Locrinus, the king of Loegria and Albany. Locrinus was the son of Brutus, a friend of King Corineus.

Gwendolyn agreed and the two began planning their wedding. But there was trouble brewing in the north of the country. Humber the Hun had invaded, and so King Locrinus said a tearful farewell to his new bride-to-be and marched north with his army to face his foe.

The battle was long, but Locrinus fought hard and was eventually victorious. He claimed all of Humber's ships and loot for himself. Hidden inside one of the ships, the king discovered a prisoner – the beautiful Princess Estrildis of Germany. On seeing Estrildis, Locrinus immediately forgot his love for Gwendolyn, who was waiting at home for his safe return. Locrinus decided to make Estrildis his wife instead.

"Make plans for a wedding," King Locrinus barked.

"But you cannot marry Estrildis!" his generals cried. "You're engaged to be married to Princess Gwendolyn. If you break the heart of King Corineus's daughter, he will ruin our kingdoms."

Locrinus knew his generals were right. But his greedy heart didn't want to let Estrildis go. Locrinus smuggled Estrildis back to his capital and ordered his men to build her a secret underground mansion full of delights and comforts.

It wasn't long until Estrildis's mansion was ready. It was filled with the richest tapestries, shiniest jewels and most expensive furniture, but she still wasn't happy.

"This is not enough," she said to Locrinus. "I deserve to be your queen, under the sun and moon in the sky. Not under the ground."

"Be patient," replied the king. "King Corineus is an old man. When he's gone, we'll be free to live as we please. I'll lock Gwendolyn up in a tower far away and you shall stand as my queen instead."

The next day, celebrations were held throughout Cornwall as Princess Gwendolyn was married to King Locrinus. The day was filled with merriment. As Queen Gwendolyn danced with her father, it was clear from her smiling face that she was unaware of her husband's secret.

Soon, both Estrildis and Queen Gwendolyn were pregnant with the king's children. Gwendolyn gave birth to a baby boy named Madden.

"You'll be a worthy successor to your father," said Queen Gwendolyn lovingly.

Hearing of Madden's birth, Estrildis realized that her daughter, Habren, would not inherit the kingdom. Sons inherited kingdoms, not daughters.

"I'll get rid of Madden," she promised Habren, and she began plotting. She commanded King Locrinus to send his wife and son far away, so Madden could never become the king's favourite child. Enchanted with Estrildis, King Locrinus agreed.

"The coastal air and your father's presence will be good for Madden," the king said, forcing Queen Gwendolyn to pack for her journey to Cornwall.

"But I don't want to travel all that way. Madden is so small. I would rather go when he is a little bigger."

But Locrinus ignored Gwendolyn's protests. After much debate, she agreed, hoping the king had their son's welfare at heart. But little did she know about cunning Estrildis and her evil plot!

After his wife and son left, King Locrinus ignored his duties as a king and spent more time underground with Estrildis and Habren.

As summers went by, Prince Madden grew up happy on the Cornish coast. Queen Gwendolyn helped her father to run his kingdom and the people of Cornwall grew to love her.

Despite this, Gwendolyn missed her life back in the capital and was eager to hear news of her husband and the kingdom. But the news she was getting wasn't good. She learned of Estrildis and Habren and their hidden mansion.

"How dare he put someone else in my place?" Gwendolyn raged. "I must teach him a lesson."

But Gwendolyn's father, King Corineus, was dying, and it was not the time for revenge. When her father passed, she and the people of Cornwall went into mourning.

Back in the capital, King Locrinus and Estrildis were overjoyed. This was the day they had been waiting for. King Locrinus dashed off a letter divorcing Gwendolyn and promptly married Princess Estrildis.

Finally free from her underground mansion, Estrildis became the queen of Loegria and Albany. Princess Habren became the heir to the throne – the throne that rightfully belonged to Prince Madden.

When the letter of divorce arrived in Cornwall, Queen Gwendolyn decided she had been patient long enough. Insulted and embarrassed, she gathered the people of Cornwall in front of her father's castle. She asked them to prepare for battle and revenge.

"I will not bear this insult quietly," she thundered. "Join me in this fight to restore justice." The people of Cornwall roared in agreement. They quickly began training, gathering supplies and repairing armour. Cornwall was ready for war.

Queen Gwendolyn put on her armour, donned her helmet and held up her sword. Before she left, she made a promise to her young son to return victorious.

"We will teach King Locrinus and his new wife a lesson," she said as she held Madden's face in her hands. "You are the rightful heir to the throne, and I will make sure that you are given everything you are owed, no matter what."

She rode at the head of her troops, determined to exact her revenge. As her army reached the banks of the River Stour, the edge of Locrinus's kingdom, Gwendolyn steadied herself and cried, "Attack!"

When news of the attack reached King Locrinus, he was not worried. In fact, he was amused.

"Gwendolyn can't fight me," he said. "She's a woman."

"But, sir, she leads a fearless and loyal army," warned his unsure generals.

King Locrinus waved them off. "I'll defeat her in a day," he boasted. Locrinus set off towards the battleground with a small troop, expecting to be back before nightfall.

But the king had misjudged his former wife's courage and skill. Gwendolyn's army pushed back. King Locrinus was losing the battle. Miserable and tired, the king sent for more troops and supplies, and Estrildis and Habren. But even they couldn't raise his spirits.

After several days of fighting, the king finally came face-to-face with Queen Gwendolyn on the battlefield. With a cry that echoed across the battleground, Queen Gwendolyn attacked King Locrinus and killed him.

Shocked and panicked, the rest of the king's army quickly surrendered. Queen Gwendolyn had fought for justice and won. But, before she marched to the capital to claim her throne, she had one more thing to do.

"Arrest Estrildis and Habren," she commanded. "There is no place for traitors in my kingdom."

Queen Gwendolyn became the queen of Loegria, Albany and Cornwall and, just as she had promised, Prince Madden became the heir to her mighty throne.

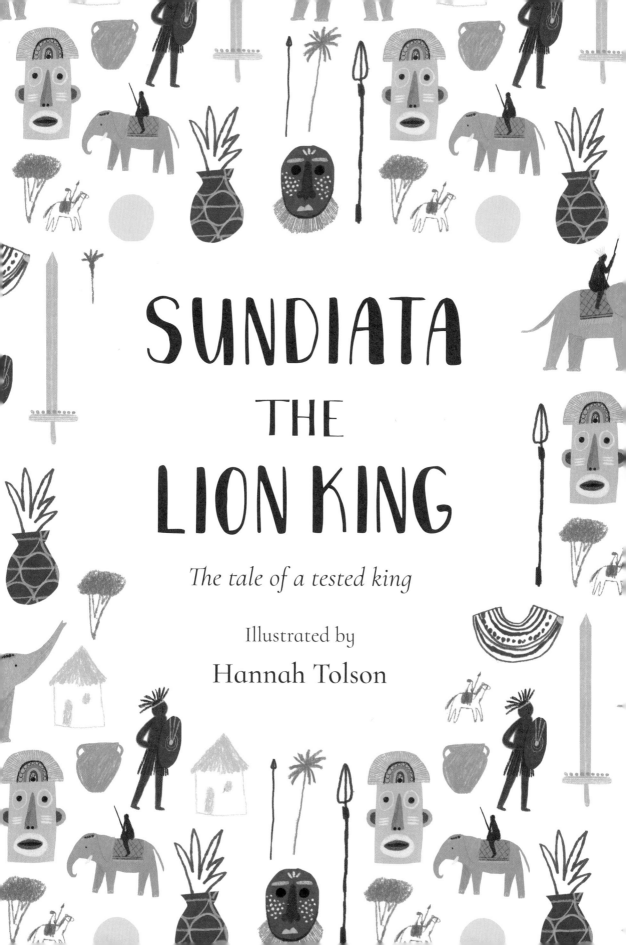

SUNDIATA
THE
LION KING

The tale of a tested king

Illustrated by

Hannah Tolson

The Manding court of King Konaté was a contented one. The king ruled alongside his wife, Sassouma, as his young son, Dankaran, played happily. But one day a fortune teller arrived, seeking an audience with the king.

"My lord," he announced, "it has been foretold that the firstborn son of a woman called Sogolon will be the greatest ruler of all time."

"Nonsense," replied the king. "My son will inherit the throne and become the greatest ruler this land has ever seen."

"That may be so," said the fortune teller, "but it is said that *only* Sogolon's son will bring power and riches to the Manding people and rule with strength and honour."

The king hesitated. He loved Sassouma more than anything but he did not want the throne to leave his bloodline. After a few days and much consultation with his advisors, Konaté summoned Sogolon to his court to marry her. He hoped to ensure that such an extraordinary child would be his.

It wasn't long before Sogolon was pregnant with her firstborn, the much-anticipated child King Konaté had been waiting for. When Sogolon gave birth to her son, Sundiata, the king was surprised. The baby was a frail and weak-looking child.

"Surely, there's been some mistake," the king cried as Sassouma and Dankaran looked on, scoffing.

Throughout his childhood, Sundiata was ridiculed. His small size and sickly appearance meant that he often stayed inside, being cared for by his loving mother.

"How could anyone think that you would ever be a strong and fearful leader?" his half-brother Dankaran teased.

It was a very lonely childhood for the young prince. But, when Sundiata was seven years old, he was invited to take part in a ceremony. This was done to mark the next stage of life for the boys – they would walk in as boys and walk out as hunters, warriors and kings.

In order to participate, Sundiata required special iron rods to be made by the local smiths to help him stand. But as he got up, ready to take part in the ceremony, the metal crutches broke in the boy's hands. Everyone ran to help Sundiata, but he refused. With his mother by his side, Sundiata stood tall for the first time in his life and his people rejoiced!

Word soon spread throughout the land that the mighty king had finally risen. Tales of Sundiata's strength and bravery spread throughout the land, almost as quickly as he grew up. Dankaran could only watch on with jealousy, as Sundiata became a great hunter and warrior, valued by his proud father for his new strength and bravery.

"You shall make a great king, Sundiata," King Konaté regularly proclaimed. "You may not be my first child, but you will inherit my throne."

Dankaran was angered by his father's words.

When King Konaté died, Dankaran realised he needed to quickly get rid of Sundiata before the people put him on the throne. The jealous prince sought out the sorcerers and together they plotted to use magic against Sundiata.

One evening, as Sundiata returned home from hunting, he came across a sorcerer, who was lying in wait. Sundiata cheerfully greeted the stranger, but the sorcerer did not respond or look Sundiata in the eyes.

"Excuse me," said the prince. "It is respectful to acknowledge someone on the same path as you."

But still, the sorcerer said nothing. Sundiata offered his elephant to the silent stranger. As the sorcerer reached out to take it, Sundiata leaned in and whispered, "I know who sent you and what you are here to do. Do it quickly."

The sorcerer was moved and he could not bring himself to harm someone with such a kind heart. Instead, he warned Sundiata to flee.

"The threats to your life will never stop," insisted the sorcerer. "Dankaran is determined and you are in danger if you stay here." Sundiata refused to leave his mother and sister, Nyakhaleng, behind so the sorcerer used his magical korte horn to summon them.

They arrived quickly and Sundiata told them everything the sorcerer had revealed to him. Panicked, the three family members began to make their plans for escape. In a few hours they were on the road, in search of safety.

The three travellers walked the dusty roads for seven long years. They were turned away or banished from many neighbouring towns, as locals feared Dankaran's wrath. Eventually, Sundiata and his mother and sister settled in the village of Djedeba, by invitation of the sorcerer king Mansa Kokon.

One day, the king summoned Sundiata to the palace to play a game of wori with him. Entering the dimly lit palace, Sundiata noticed the impressive weapons that were hanging on display.

"Boy, you have come," the king said to Sundiata. "The rules are simple. If you lose, you die. If you win –"

"I get that sword," Sundiata interrupted. He pointed to the largest sword in the collection. The king agreed. As the two sat down to play the game with pebbles and sorcery, King Mansa recited a poem.

When it was Sundiata's turn, he continued the king's poem, adding the line, "But the gold came only yesterday." King Mansa looked up at the boy. How could he know?

"My father's first wife, Sassouma, sent you gold to kill me, didn't she?" asked Sundiata calmly. The king, astonished he had been found out, immediately dismissed the boy and then banished the family from his lands. And so they travelled on.

The family finally settled in Mema for many years without any trouble. But there was misfortune back at home.

One day, a messenger arrived in search of the lost prince. "Sundiata, I have been wandering for months in search of you. I bring news of the Manding people. One by one, your brothers, including Dankaran, have been made king. And, one by one, the sorcerer Sumanguru Kante has defeated them. You are our only hope."

Sundiata knew that he would have to go to war for his people, but he would not leave his greatest ally, his mother. "My mother is not strong enough to travel. She has been sick for many days and I fear the worst is to come. She has done so much for me; I must be here for her."

"Son," Sogolon said, "you must put our people above your own needs. That is what a king would do."

Sundiata was heartbroken to leave his mother but he knew that she was right, just as she had been his whole life. So Sundiata and Nyakhaleng began their journey back towards the kingdom they had run from for so long. Finally, they reached the city of Dakhajala, the last city on the map before Manding.

Sundiata appealed to his allies for help – he needed an army to follow him into the battlefield. Thousands of warriors pledged to join this lost and legendary king, known for his lion-like strength and bravery. If *he* was going to battle, victory must be certain.

Sundiata's army fought a long battle against the sorcerer Sumanguru Kante. Sundiata fought with skill and strength, but Sumanguru fought with skill and magic. Finally, Nyakhaleng came up with a plan.

She knew that if she could find out how to defeat Sumanguru, she could help her brother. Nyakhaleng decided she would travel across the enemy lines and visit Sumanguru.

Sumanguru was surprised to see his enemy's sister. *I will hear what she wants*, he thought. *Then I will slay her.*

Nyakhaleng told the sorcerer that she had turned against her brother and wanted to be with someone who appreciated her. Sumanguru did not believe Nyakhaleng at first, suspecting her of trickery. But the longer he spent with her, the more she convinced him that she was to be believed.

"Mighty sorcerer, my brother is not the lion king that was foretold by the fortune teller all those years ago," she said. "I have been by his side for years and I can tell you that he is still the weak child he was at heart. He can be no match for you."

"But of course," replied the arrogant Sumanguru, who had started to fall in love with the well-spoken princess. "Even more when he realizes that I am protected by my father's magic. He is a mighty jinn who lives in the mountains. No one can defeat me, especially your mortal brother, while my father lives."

That night, Nyakhaleng slipped away from the palace to report back to her grateful brother, Sundiata.

Upon learning that Sumanguru was untouchable while his father was still alive, Sundiata and his armies went in search of the jinn in the mountains.

They soon found the cave belonging to the jinn and quietly built a campfire outside the entrance. Sundiata's soldiers fanned smoke into the cave. Using the smoke as a cover, Sundiata walked into the dark tunnel, bow and arrow in hand.

Sundiata had heard that the invisible jinn could be seen as a shadow through smoke and it wasn't long before Sundiata's arrow found its target.

Returning victorious from the mountains, Sundiata turned to pursue the sorcerer who had held the kingdom in terror for so long.

But Sumanguru had sensed his father's protection fall away and knew that, without it, Sundiata would be victorious. Feeling scared and vulnerable, the sorcerer quickly transformed into a Senegalese coucal. Soaring high above his enemies, the bird Sumanguru flew to the hills for safety and was never seen again.

With his sister's help, Sundiata had defeated the evil sorcerer and set his people free. He became ruler of the Manding and created the Mali Empire, which prospered for centuries.

"UNEASY LIES

THAT

A

THE HEAD WEARS CROWN"

Shakespeare's *Henry IV, Part II* (III.i.31)

LADYBIRD BOOKS

UK | USA | Canada | Ireland | Australia
India | New Zealand | South Africa

Ladybird Books is part of the Penguin Random House group of companies
whose addresses can be found at global.penguinrandomhouse.com

www.penguin.co.uk   www.puffin.co.uk   www.ladybird.co.uk

First published 2020
001

Introduction by Gemma Whelan
"The Sword in the Stone" retold by Yvonne Battle-Felton, illustrated by Martina Heiduczek
"Yennenga and the Mossi Kingdom" retold by Yvonne Battle-Felton, illustrated by Lidia Tomashevskaya
"Rostam and Rakhsh" retold by Chitra Soundar, illustrated by Pham Quang Phuc
"Shakuntala" retold by Chitra Soundar, illustrated by Alheteia Straathof
"Gwendolyn and Locrinus" retold by Chitra Soundar, illustrated by Kirsti Davidson
"Sundiata, the Lion King" retold by Yvonne Battle-Felton, illustrated by Hannah Tolson
Copyright © Ladybird Books Ltd, 2020

Printed in China

A CIP catalogue record for this book is available from the British Library

ISBN: 978–0–241–41358–6

All correspondence to:
Ladybird Books
Penguin Random House Children's
One Embassy Gardens, 8 Viaduct Gardens, London SW11 7BW